The Courtship of the
YONGHY-BONGHY-BÒ
& THE NEW VESTMENTS

EDWARD LEAR

The Courtship of the YONGHY-BONGHY-BÒ & THE NEW VESTMENTS

Illustrated by Kevin Maddison

A Studio Book
The Viking Press
New York

Illustrations Copyright © Kevin Maddison 1980

Published in 1980 by The Viking Press
625 Madison Avenue, New York, N.Y. 10022

Published simultaneously in Canada by
Penguin Books Canada Limited

Produced by Ash & Grant
9 Henrietta Street, London WC2E 8PS

Library of Congress Cataloging in Publication Data

Lear, Edward, 1812-1888
   The courtship of The Yonghy-Bonghy-Bò and the new
vestments.

   (A Studio book)
   Summary: The first nonsense poem tells the tale of
the Yonghy-Bonghy-Bò's unsuccessful courtship; the
second describes the devouring, by a menagerie of
animals, of an old man's unusual costume made of food.
   1. Nonsense verses, England.   [1. Nonsense verses.
2. English poetry]   I. Lear, Edward, 1812-1888.   The
new vestments.   II. Maddison, Kevin.   III. Title.
IV. Title: The new vestments.
PZ8.3.L477Co   1979   821'.8   79-14309

ISBN 0-670-24428-7

Printed in Holland

The Yonghy-Bonghy-Bò

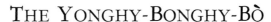

On the coast of Co-ro-man-del, Where the ear-ly pumpkins grow, In the middle of the woods, Lived the Yonghy Bonghy Bò, Two old chairs and half a candle, One old jug without a handle, These were all his worldly goods, In the middle of the woods, These were all the world-ly goods, Of the Yonghy Bonghy Bò, Of the Yong-hy Bong-hy Bò.

The Air of the Song by Edward Lear;
the Arrangement for the Piano by Professor Pomè, of Sanremo, Italy.

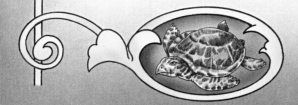

On the Coast of Coromandel
Where the early pumpkins blow,
In the middle of the woods
Lived the Yonghy-Bonghy-Bò.
Two old chairs, and half a candle,—
One old jug without a handle,—
These were all his worldly goods:
In the middle of the woods,
These were all the worldly goods,
Of the Yonghy-Bonghy-Bò,
Of the Yonghy-Bonghy-Bò.

Once, among the Bong-trees walking
Where the early pumpkins blow,
To a little heap of stones
Came the Yonghy-Bonghy-Bò.
There he heard a Lady talking,
To some milk-white Hens of Dorking,—
''Tis the Lady Jingly Jones!
'On that little heap of stones
'Sits the Lady Jingly Jones!'
Said the Yonghy-Bonghy-Bò,
Said the Yonghy-Bonghy-Bò.

'Lady Jingly! Lady Jingly!
'Sitting where the pumpkins blow,
'Will you come and be my wife?'
 Said the Yonghy-Bonghy-Bò.
'I am tired of living singly,—
'On this coast so wild and shingly,—
'I'm a-weary of my life:
'If you'll come and be my wife,
'Quite serene would be my life!'—
 Said the Yonghy-Bonghy-Bò,
 Said the Yonghy-Bonghy-Bò.

'On this Coast of Coromandel,
'Shrimps and watercresses grow,
'Prawns are plentiful and cheap,'
  Said the Yonghy-Bonghy-Bò.
'You shall have my Chairs and candle,
'And my jug without a handle!—
'Gaze upon the rolling deep
('Fish is plentiful and cheap)
 'As the sea, my love is deep!'
  Said the Yonghy-Bonghy-Bò,
  Said the Yonghy-Bonghy-Bò.

Lady Jingly answered sadly,
  And her tears began to flow,—
'Your proposal comes too late,
'Mr. Yonghy-Bonghy-Bò!
'I would be your wife most gladly!'
(Here she twirled her fingers madly,)
'But in England I've a mate!
'Yes! you've asked me far too late,
'For in England I've a mate,
'Mr. Yonghy-Bonghy-Bò!
'Mr. Yonghy-Bonghy-Bò!'

'Mr. Jones — (his name is Handel,—
'Handel Jones, Esquire, & Co.)
'Dorking fowls delights to send,
'Mr. Yonghy-Bonghy-Bò!
'Keep, oh! keep your chairs and candle,
'And your jug without a handle,—
'I can merely be your friend!
'— Should my Jones more Dorkings send,
'I will give you three, my friend!
'Mr. Yonghy-Bonghy-Bò!
'Mr. Yonghy-Bonghy-Bò!'

'Though you've such a tiny body,
'And your head so large doth grow,—
'Though your hat may blow away,
'Mr. Yonghy-Bonghy-Bò!
'Though you're such a Hoddy Doddy—
'Yet I wish that I could modi-
'fy the words I needs must say!
'Will you please to go away?
'That is all I have to say—
'Mr. Yonghy-Bonghy-Bò!
'Mr. Yonghy-Bonghy-Bò!'

Down the slippery slopes of Myrtle,
Where the early pumpkins blow,
To the calm and silent sea
Fled the Yonghy-Bonghy-Bò.
There, beyond the Bay of Gurtle,
Lay a large and lively Turtle;—
'You're the Cove,' he said, 'for me
'On your back beyond the sea,
'Turtle, you shall carry me!'
Said the Yonghy-Bonghy-Bò,
Said the Yonghy-Bonghy-Bò.

Through the silent-roaring ocean
Did the Turtle swiftly go;
Holding fast upon his shell
Rode the Yonghy-Bonghy-Bò.
With a sad primæval motion
Towards the sunset isles of Boshen
Still the Turtle bore him well.
Holding fast upon his shell,
'Lady Jingly Jones, farewell!'
Sang the Yonghy-Bonghy-Bò,
Sang the Yonghy-Bonghy-Bò.

From the Coast of Coromandel,
Did that Lady never go;
On that heap of stones she mourns
For the Yonghy-Bonghy-Bò.
On that Coast of Coromandel,
In his jug without a handle
Still she weeps, and daily moans;
On that little heap of stones
To her Dorking Hens she moans,
For the Yonghy-Bonghy-Bò,
For the Yonghy-Bonghy-Bò.

THE NEW VESTMENTS

There lived an old man in the Kingdom of Tess,
Who invented a purely original dress;
And when it was perfectly made and complete,
He opened the door, and walked into the street.

By way of a hat, he'd a loaf of Brown Bread,
In the middle of which he inserted his head;—
His Shirt was made up of no end of dead Mice,
The warmth of whose skins was quite fluffy and nice;—
His Drawers were of Rabbit-skins;—so were his Shoes;—
His Stockings were skins,—but it is not known whose;—
His Waistcoat and Trowsers were made of Pork Chops;—
His Buttons were Jujubes, and Chocolate Drops;—
His Coat was all Pancakes with Jam for a border,
And a girdle of Biscuits to keep it in order;
And he wore over all, as a screen from bad weather,
A Cloak of green Cabbage-leaves stitched all together.

He had walked a short way, when he heard a great noise,
Of all sorts of Beasticles, Birdlings, and Boys;—
And from every long street and dark lane in the town
Beasts, Birdles, and Boys in a tumult rushed down.
Two Cows and a half ate his Cabbage-leaf Cloak;—
Four Apes seized his Girdle, which vanished like smoke;—
Three Kids ate up half of his Pancaky Coat,—
And the tails were devour'd by an ancient He Goat;—
An army of Dogs in a twinkling tore *up* his
Pork Waistcoat and Trowsers to give to their Puppies;—
And while they were growling, and mumbling the Chops,
Ten Boys prigged the Jujubes and Chocolate Drops.—
He tried to run back to his house, but in vain,
For Scores of fat Pigs came again and again;—
They rushed out of stables and hovels and doors,—
They tore off his stockings, his shoes, and his drawers;—
And now from the housetops with screechings descend,
Striped, spotted, white, black, and gray Cats without end,
They jumped on his shoulders and knocked off his hat,—
When Crows, Ducks, and Hens made a mincemeat of that;—
They speedily flew at his sleeves in a trice,
And utterly tore up his Shirt of dead Mice;—
They swallowed the last of his Shirt with a squall,—
Whereon he ran home with no clothes on at all.

And he said to himself as he bolted the door,
'I will not wear a similar dress any more,
'Any more, any more, any more, never more!'